Amos and Abraham

Written by Sharyn Bellafiore
Illustrated by Steve Myers

Good Books®

Intercourse, PA 17534

Amos could not wait. His friend April was bringing her cousin Abraham to the farm for a visit. April said Abraham lived in the city, but he wanted to learn all about country life.

Amos had lived all his life on a farm. Amos was Old Order Amish. His pop, Daniel, farmed and made their family's living by selling milk from their cows to nearby dairies.

Amos' school had only one room. At school he spoke English, but at home he and his family talked Pennsylvania Dutch. He and his four brothers and three sisters each had chores to do. But they always had time for visiting, and tomorrow was a special day.

Not only were April and Abraham visiting the farm, but then they would all go back to April's house to play with her animals. Amos had a lot of animals on his farm but he didn't have two silly dogs like April's. And he certainly didn't have a green lizard named Murry!

Abraham could not wait. He was on his way to visit his cousin April in the country. Abraham lived in the city and went to a Hebrew Academy. In school he spoke Yiddish and English. He and his three brothers and two sisters belonged to the Hasidic Jewish community. April was his cousin, but she was not as orthodox as he was.

Visiting April in the country was one of his favorite things, especially playing with her two silly dogs. Then there was her lizard Murry!

Abraham especially liked when Murry sat on his head! April told him that was Murry's favorite position because it gave him the best view of the world.

This time April promised Abraham a special surprise. She was going to take him out to the country to meet her Amish friend Amos. Amos was exactly the same age as Abraham.

Abraham—at April's house, and Amos—on the farm, were
both a little nervous. But when Amos saw the car drive down the
lane, he ran to greet the visitors.

"Hello," both boys said shyly at the same time. "Would you like to help me milk the cows?" Amos asked. Abraham grinned and galloped along beside him to the barn.

"Don't forget to watch where you step!" yelled April.

April was right. There *were* a lot of places to step over and around. Amos took Abraham to the barn and introduced him to his herd of black and white Holstein cows. Amos and his brothers milked them twice each day. Before they began, they washed the cows' udders. Then they attached the milking machines.

Although Amos' family didn't milk by hand, Amos showed Abraham how to do it. Nothing came at first—but suddenly, after one hard squeeze, milk squirted out! Abraham laughed. He was afraid he would hurt the cow. "No chance," said Amos. "Lilac would be terribly uncomfortable if she wasn't milked."

Abraham could hardly believe that most cows on Amos' farm give five gallons of milk each day. That's 20 quarts, as much as Abraham's family drinks in one month.

"Come around to the back of the barn," called Amos. Lying tucked against the pen was a calf, just a few days old. Amos said that when it was born, the baby weighed about 100 pounds.

When she saw the boys, Dandelion wobbled to her feet and began sucking on a pacifier attached to a pail. Amos said the newborn calf drank its mother's milk for a few days. Then Amos' pop gave it a milk substitute. Since Dandelion wanted to suck, the pail was a special one with a pacifier attached. "That way we can sell Dandelion's mother's milk to the local dairy," explained Amos.

"Do you want to feel something funny?" Amos asked. "Let Dandelion suck your fingers. Don't worry, she won't bite."

It was a tingly wet funny feeling. Abraham discovered that cows have front teeth only on the bottoms of their mouths. And so they have very large tongues which they use to pull grass and other food into their mouths.

"Get this," said Amos to Abraham. "Cows have four stomachs. Did you ever hear that they chew their cuds? Well, that's because they keep redigesting their food for about eight hours each day."

A rooster set up a squawk as the two boys headed out of the barn. "Hey, I thought they only do that in the morning," said Abraham.

"They do it all day long," answered Amos. "He's announcing that we're walking through his territory."

Two goats lived along Amos' lane. "We milk Kick and Flick," he told Abraham. "Watch the candy and the paper in your pockets. They're not after tin cans, but they'll find those other goodies if you have them!"

The floppy-eared goats looked a little like rabbits to Abraham.

"Cows graze, but goats browse," said Amos. "Mom doesn't want them near the washline! They think all those swaying shirts are theirs to play with! Mom only puts up with Kick and Flick because their milk is good to drink—and we use it for making cheese."

"How do you stand all these awful farm smells?" Abraham's nose was in a knot!

Amos' nose moved into a snoot. "How do you stand all those awful city smells? The bus fumes are the worst! At least our farm smells help the crops grow!"

Their next stop was the chicken house. Abraham opened the door and walked in. Feathers flew, wings flapped wildly, and the chickens rushed to all the corners at the same time.

"You have to knock first," laughed Amos. "Every day I hunt the eggs. Each chicken lays one each day. Ours give white eggs, but some give brown."

"How about a buggy ride?" Amos asked Abraham as they dusted themselves off from the stir of the chicken house. Amos made sense out of the tangle of straps and reins, and then hitched prancing Rhubarb to the gray carriage. The boys climbed in and Rhubarb took off down the back lane.

"Do you have a license?" Abraham wondered.

"No, we don't need to have one. But Pop and Mom make sure we know how to drive safely," said Amos. "This is my first summer to drive alone. And I'm allowed only on the back roads."

"Why do you put covers over the horse's eyes?" asked Abraham.

"Horses shouldn't look around when they drive. If they do, they get distracted by what they're passing," explained Amos. "I wouldn't mind blinders myself, sometimes, especially when those big trucks whip by." His grin had a touch of disgust.

"Must you dress a certain way?" Amos asked Abraham as Rhubarb pulled them along the lane.

"I dress very plain now," Abraham pointed to his side curls and simple plaid shirt, "but when I get a little older, I'll dress even more plain, like my ancestors did. I must always wear a head covering, *a yarmulke,* then, and I will let my sideburns, my *pais,* grow."

"Do you ever feel different and that people are looking at you?" Amos glanced away from Rhubarb's trotting back and over at Abraham.

"Yup," Abraham nodded, never hesitating.

"Me, too," Amos grinned. "But, you know, when I'm with other Amish, I don't think about being different. And when I'm with my family, I think other people dress awfully strange! *Ja, well.*"

"Do you know Yiddish?" Abraham took a quick look at Amos.

"Neh, that was Pennsylvania Dutch."

"Sure sounded like Yiddish to me!" Abraham zipped off a whole row of Yiddish.

Amos took a turn with Pennsylvania Dutch. The buggy rocked as the boys laughed out their languages, now and then so similar, yet always too different to be sure of what the other was saying!

"Do you mind not having electricity? Or television? Or video games?" Abraham asked.

"We've never had all that so I don't miss it," Amos said, thinking about how his life could be different than it was. "We're so busy with our farm and each other, we'd never have time for all those things."

Abraham didn't watch *much* TV, but he wasn't sure he could give it up the whole way. He looked at Amos carefully, surprised that he could accept his church's ideas about how to live, especially when it asked hard things. But Amos was happy, Abraham could see that.

"See what happened while you were gone," Amos' pop smiled at the boys when they got back to the barn. He pointed toward the pig pen.

Amos climbed in next to the mother pig and her 10 new babies. Amos took the warm wiggly piglets and put each one by the mother pig's teats. Every little mouth took hold. Abraham had never heard such snorting.

"Have you fellas been out to check on the lambs yet?" Amos' pop asked when the pigs were all drinking.

"Blackberry needs his bottle. Maybe Abraham could feed him while you keep his nosy cousins away, Amos."

Amos swung by the milk house to fill up the bottle for the skinny charcoal lamb.

Blackberry raced around the legs of the rowdy larger lambs playing in the meadow. "They were all born this spring, but we kept Blackberry in the kitchen till he grew big enough to not get run over by the others. He was the tiny twin; almost too little to live. I usually feed him so he knows me pretty well."

Amos climbed over the fence and into the meadow. "Come on," he called to Abraham. "I'll catch him; then you try to feed him while I play tag with the other guys. That way he can eat in peace."

Abraham gathered the warm wooly body against himself. He set Blackberry down and the busy little lamb grabbed hold of the nipple. While he drank, he looked straight into Abraham's eyes.

"Would you like to take Blackberry home and raise him til he's big enough to keep our grass short and wooly enough to have his coat clipped?"

"Sorry. The neighbors above us and below us and beside us would run us right out of our building," laughed Abraham.

"Well, then, I'll just raise him myself, and the next time you come, I'll show you how calm he's become. And I'll save you some of his first wool."

A chance to visit Amos and his farm again! And maybe a sweater made from Blackberry's wool. Abraham could hardly believe this day was happening.

"Those bird houses sure do look like condominiums," Abraham pointed to the houses with many layers, perched on poles in the garden.

"They're for purple martins. They like community housing," smiled Amos. "We like them to live beside our garden because they keep the bugs under control. Watch them use their beaks like a scoop as they fly along, gathering up insects."

"Whew, I'd like to attract a few of those to the city on hot nights when the mosquitoes are biting," said Abraham.

Suddenly Abraham heard a honking blast. He turned around to discover a flock of geese, gaining ground behind him.

"Run!" yelled Amos. "The geese think you're an intruder and they're the watchdogs."

The boys landed safely on the porch where Pop, Mom, Benuel, Sam, Sadie Mae, Elizabeth, Jake, Mose, Lydia—and April—stood watching. And laughing.

"Time to go," said April. Amos and Abraham took off for the back seat.

"Just a minute. I thought you didn't ride in cars," Abraham suddenly stopped.

"We don't own cars. But we may ride in them," answered Amos as he ducked in the back door.

"Take us to Murry and the dogs, April!" directed Abraham.

April watched them through the rear view mirror, happy that Amos and Abraham had discovered each other. "Two boys so similar, yet so very different," she thought.

Bagel, the beagle, and Clover, the basset hound, leaped all over Amos and Abraham when they walked into April's house. "At least here we don't have to watch where we step," grinned Abraham. "Let's take 'em for a walk."

"Bring Murry!" squealed Amos.

About the Author

Sharyn Bellafiore lives in Lancaster, Pennsylvania, with her husband Dennis, daughter April, two dogs, and Murry the lizard. She is on the board of directors of the Lancaster Jewish Community Center and is a member of Degel Israel Congregation.

She is a former teacher who has worked as a tour guide for years.

About the Illustrator

Steve Myers is an advertising art director and designer working in Lancaster, Pennsylvania. He also works as a freelance commercial illustrator and fine artist, and has exhibited in numerous shows throughout the area. Steve attended the Rhode Island School of Design, majoring in illustration.

About the Old Order Amish and the Hasidic Jews

Because several Amish communities lie close to major cities where Hasidic Jews live, it is entirely possible that an Amish Amos and a Jewish Abraham could meet.

For more information about the Amish write to The People's Place, Box 419, Intercourse, PA 17534. The People's Place is an educational center, interpreting the Amish and Mennonites.

For more information about Hasidic Jews write to the Lubavitch Youth Organization, 305 Kingston Ave., Brooklyn, N.Y. 11213, or call 718/953-1000.

AMOS AND ABRAHAM
Copyright © 1994 by Good Books, Intercourse, PA 17534
Design by Dawn J. Ranck
International Standard Book Number: 1-56148-139-4
Library of Congress Catalog Card Number: 94-33000

Library of Congress Cataloging-in-Publication Data

Bellafiore, Sharyn.
   Amos and Abraham / written by Sharyn Bellafiore : illustrated by Steve Myers.
      p. cm.
   Summary: Abraham, a young Jewish boy, becomes friends with Amos, a young Amish boy, during a visit to Amos' farm.
      ISBN 1-56148-139-4
      [1. Amish--Fiction. 2. Jews--United States--Fiction. 3. Farm life--Fiction.] I. Myers, Steve, ill. II. Title.
   PZ7.B4125Am   1994
   [Fic]--dc20   94-33000
                                                                              CIP
                                                                              AC